The Christmas Curse of Krampus

Gruss Vom Krampus!

Devin Arloski

Devin Arloski

The Christmas Curse Of Krampus
Published by EurownAmerica Publishing
Longmont, CO

Copyright © 2022 by Devin Arloski. All rights reserved.

No part of this book may be reproduced in any form or by any mechanical means, including information storage and retrieval systems without permission in writing from the publisher/author, except by a reviewer who may quote passages in a review.

All images, logos, quotes, and trademarks included in this book are subject to use according to trademark and copyright laws of the United States of America.

Publisher's Cataloging-in-Publication data

Names: Arloski, Devin, author.
Title: The Christmas Curse of Krampus / Devin Arloski.
Description: Longmont, CO: EurownAmerica Publishing, 2022.| Summary: Santa needs Max's help to defeat Krampus and save Christmas as well as restore Max's belief in Christmas and family.
Identifiers: ISBN: 978-0-578-95239-0
Subjects: LCSH Santa Claus--Juvenile fiction. | Krampus--Juvenile fiction. | Christmas stories. | BISAC JUVENILE FICTION / Holidays & Celebrations / Christmas & Advent
Classification: LCC PZ7.1.A745 Ch 2022 | DDC [Fic]--dc23

ISBN: 978-0-578-95239-0
JUVENILE FICTION / Holidays & Celebrations / Christmas & Advent

Cover and Interior design by Victoria Wolf, wolfdesignandmarketing.com, copyright owned by Devin Arloski.

Illustrations by James Hutton.

QUANTITY PURCHASES: Schools, companies, professional groups, clubs, and other organizations may qualify for special terms when ordering quantities of this title. For information, email darloski7@gmail.com

All rights reserved by Devin Arloski and EurownAmerica Publishing.
Printed in the United States of America.

For Sara, Barrett, and Cameron. May you always leave your hearts open to wonderment and whimsy...

Contents

Chapter 1: All alone 1

Chapter 2: A locket to remember her by 5

Chapter 3: The Christmas market 9

Chapter 4: Krampus 13

Chapter 5: The Weihnachtsmann and the Woodlings 17

Chapter 6: Dreams of Christmas past 21

Chapter 7: A cabin in the snow 25

Chapter 8: Santa's reindeer 29

Chapter 9: A call to action 33

Chapter 10: Darklings 37

Chapter 11: Terror at the Krampuslauf 41

Chapter 12: Buried alive 45

Chapter 13: The Lutzelfrau 49

Chapter 14: The naughty list 53

Chapter 15: Making toys 57

Chapter 16: A technological solution 61

Chapter 17: The Nachtkrapp ... 65

Chapter 18: Krampus at the gates ... 69

Chapter 19: The plan to save Christmas ... 73

Chapter 20: Christmas chemistry ... 77

Chapter 21: Back to civilization ... 81

Chapter 22: Discovered by Darklings ... 85

Chapter 23: Krampus's lair ... 89

Chapter 24: Food cage! ... 93

Chapter 25: A joyous reunion ... 97

Chapter 26: The sleigh ... 101

Chapter 27: Delivering presents ... 105

Chapter 28: An unwelcome surprise ... 109

Chapter 29: The meaning of Christmas spirit ... 113

About the Author ... 117

Chapter 1:

All Alone

Max didn't believe in Santa Claus anymore. He was eleven now, and it was silly to think that a jolly old man in a red suit flew around the world delivering presents to all the children on earth in just one night. It was fun to believe in the magic when he was younger, but Christmas hadn't been the same for the last several years.

Max spent his days zoning out on his tablet or his dad's computer, playing video games. He could spend hours and hours on it, and his dad really didn't care or wasn't around to notice. Otherwise, he was at school and under the watchful eye of Fraulein Heimlich, a German woman who shouted at him in her native tongue every day. Being in Germany was strange. Max didn't have any friends or understand their language, and the food was gross and bizarre. Max was the maddest he had ever been at his dad for this most recent move to Germany after a string of other moves over the years. "Military families need to expect and accept moves regularly," is what most adults told him when he complained about it.

Christmas was only twenty days away, and it seemed like it would be a day just like any other. While other kids were with their brothers, sisters, parents, and grandparents, opening presents and doing all the fun Christmas celebrations and stuff, for Max, it was just him and his dad. He didn't have any relatives other than an uncle whom his dad didn't keep in touch with. Max's dad would probably buy something at the military base gift shop "wrapped" in a brown paper bag and try to pass it off as a gift from Santa. The only gifts Max wanted were new video games, but he knew his dad had no idea which ones Max even wanted.

"Jung Max!" Fraulein Heimlich shouted. "Pay attention when I'm talking to you!" Max understood a sentence here or there but winced when she yelled close to his ears. At times, he could smell her hot, stinky breath on his neck, and it made him cringe.

"And quit biting your fingernails," she insisted. Unfortunately, this military base was so small that they didn't have a school on the base, so he had to attend a German school in a nearby town. He escaped into his daydreams during classes, passing the hours until he could get back to his computer. Max was hooked on a new game called *War of the Planets*, and he only needed to kill three hundred more intergalactic soldiers to make it to the next level. This would reveal a cool, new mystery weapon upgrade. It was all he could think about. Max felt important when he played it, like he was really needed and wanted. His friends back in the United States were part of his online team, and playing online offered a way to keep in touch with them, even though he didn't consider any of them close friends. They were counting on him, and playing the game enabled him to forget that he hated life in Germany. He could forget anything related to the fact that Christmas was coming and forget about everything outside the military base apartment.

"Are you listening to me, Jung Max?" Fraulein Heimlich shouted again.

Max hadn't been, of course, and all he could muster to say was, "Uh-huh."

She gave him an exasperated look and then continued to address the class.

"Today, we will be writing a letter to Father Christmas, the Weihnachtsmann. Please include your toy list, and I will send them to the North Pole," she instructed.

"What a waste of time," Max blurted out, not thinking. *Uh oh, that is going to cost me.*

"Jung Max, to the Schullieter now!" she shouted. He knew that word; he heard it so often, it seemed like a daily occurrence. It was the principal's office. Max slowly rose from his chair and slouched his way out of the classroom and down the hall. He waited in the principal's office for what seemed like an eternity, thinking about why he had said what he did. He just wanted someone to talk to, someone who understood him. Maybe it was a cry for attention. Deep down, he felt bad for making a scene in class, and even though he didn't believe in Santa anymore, he was sure his classmates still did.

The secretary spoke in broken English, "Max, your father is on zee way to pick you up, take you back home."

After a few more minutes, his dad arrived and gave Max a cold stare before being led into the principal's office to discuss "the problem with Max." He heard them talking and the principal yelling and then Max's dad emerged from the office and took Max by the arm to the car. They didn't speak a word the whole way back. For

Max, the silence was worse than if he were being yelled at. His dad used to get angry and yell at him, but he had given up a while ago. It was as if he thought nothing could be done for Max now. It certainly didn't help that Max's grades were the lowest they had ever been. There was talk that he may even have to repeat a grade, not because he wasn't smart but because he didn't care and didn't do the work. Max felt hollow in the pit of his stomach. *Whatever*, thought Max, brushing off this feeling. He would be online soon and able to talk to his friends. Hopefully, this would lift his spirits.

Chapter 2:

A Locket to Remember Her By

When they finally made it back to the apartment, the internet was down, and Max couldn't play his game. *Of all the days to have the internet be down, it had to be today*, Max thought. He used to have *War of the Planets* foam dart guns but had lost them and hadn't bothered looking for them since the video game was so much more fun. He didn't have any friends to play it with anyway. The boredom was unbearable. Most of his other toys didn't interest him anymore. Books either. He would have to try to watch TV until his dad finished up paperwork in his office. But German TV was terrible, and the apartment didn't have a satellite dish that could bring in English channels yet. Strange shows in a language he couldn't understand would only hold his attention for a few minutes. Really? A TV show about making Limburger cheese?

"What are we going to do, Wilbur?" he said as he softly stroked the back of his fat orange cat, hoping Wilbur would somehow answer him. With nothing to do and no answer from his cat, Max began thinking about his predicament and his mom and dad. Even though he wasn't happy in Germany and missed his friends back home, he still loved his dad. But lately, since his mom had been missing for the past three years, he felt disconnected from his dad and blamed him for everything that happened leading up to their arrival in Germany. His mom had left for a business trip to Belgium and simply never returned. His dad had told Max that he accepted the post in Germany to be closer to where she disappeared so he could search for her. But life had gone on for some time now, and nothing had changed. It didn't help that his dad was constantly yelling at Max and always seemed sad or angry. He pulled out a heart-shaped silver locket from a drawer in his room and stared as it spun at the end of a chain. It was old and had beautiful, engraved markings on it. A memory flash came to him of his mom cutting a small piece of her hair and placing it inside the locket.

"Here, take this, so you always have a piece of me with you," she said. He felt as though he might cry, but as quickly as the memory came to him, it was gone. Just like his mom.

"Max!" his dad yelled. "I told you to empty the garbage five times! Why haven't you done it?"

"I don't know how," Max whined in a pathetic voice.

"You do know how, you just don't *want* to," his dad replied angrily.

"Okay fine! I don't want to then," Max snapped back.

"Get back in your room now, mister," his dad insisted.

Max played with his Legos for an hour or so before his dad finally came into the bedroom.

"C'mon, get your coat. We're going out." *He must be over our argument now. Maybe getting out of the house together will make us feel a little better,* Max thought.

Chapter 3:
The Christmas Market

THE TOWN OF DINKELSTADT was right on the Austrian/German border and not far from the military base where his dad worked. They arrived just as the sun was setting. The entire town was lit up for the Christmas holiday, and Max had never seen anything like it. Christmas lights were everywhere, so bright they nearly blinded him. Crowds filled the streets, and the smell of gingerbread cookies and roasted chestnuts hung in the air. Little wooden stalls were all lined up, selling toys, crafts, candy, cookies and assorted trinkets. He could hear people singing carols. The sounds of bells ringing and children laughing completed the symphony of his senses. It looked, sounded and smelled like a scene from a fairytale. *Christmas is stupid*, Max thought, but all that stuff *did* look like fun. Max's dad leaned over and said, "Listen Max, I miss mom, too, you know. I know you're not happy with me or the move here, but let's try to have some fun tonight, okay?" Max rolled his eyes and didn't respond.

"I bet we can find a pretzel and something to drink." *A pretzel? What is so special about a pretzel?*

"Mom always used to get me ice cream. If she were still here, she would get me ice cream," Max whined.

"You're getting a pretzel, and that's that," his father snapped. He bought Max a huge chewy pretzel and hot chocolate. The size of the pretzel surprised Max, and when he bit into it, he tried to hide his delight from his dad but caught himself vocalizing his enjoyment.

"Mmmm."

"Still want ice cream instead?" his father asked.

While Max was enjoying the pretzel and hot chocolate, his father got some weird drink called "Gluhwein." Max didn't think it was possible to make wine out of glue or why anyone would want to, but there it was in nearly every stall. It wasn't a drink for kids, and it sounded disgusting, so Max didn't give it another thought.

There was so much to see and do in Dinkelstadt. Max got to throw a hatchet and shoot a bow and arrow at a target. He and his father rode a Christmas-themed train and then a beautifully decorated carousel. Max's dad was smiling when they rode the carousel, and Max hadn't seen his dad smile in a long time. Max couldn't help it, and a smile came over his face too. After riding the carousel, they ate gingerbread cookies and chocolate-shaped Weihnachtsmann in the shape of Santa Claus. Everything was delicious, and all of the sights and sounds were magical. It felt foreign to him, and although he was trying hard to hide it, he was having fun.

Suddenly, Max found himself thinking several years back when Christmas was still a time of joy for him. He was opening presents on Christmas morning with his parents back in their home in the US. He had run down the stairs, wondering with eager anticipation what Santa had brought for him. Tearing the wrapping paper off in a frenzy, he had shown his parents all of the wonderful toys he had been waiting to play with for months.

When he came back to his senses, Max looked around to find that he was all alone. *Where is my dad? How long have I been daydreaming?* Panic began to set in as he ran from stall to stall, asking the vendors for help. But no one understood him. The small town seemed vast and never-ending. He remembered two German words his dad had taught him, "hilfe" (help) and "bitte" (please). Max's limited German vocabulary only confused the townspeople.

When he was past the last stall, he came to the edge of a forest. He was about to turn back when his eyes noticed a strange light emanating from the forest. He had seen plenty of lights that night, but this one was different. The suspicious light glowed with a mysterious appearance that seemed more like a fire. Max found that the light was somehow calming him, almost beckoning him. As if his legs had a mind of their own, he entered the dark, cold woods.

Chapter 4:

Krampus

THE COAT HIS DAD HAD GIVEN HIM was meant for winters in Virginia back in the US and was hardly adequate for the Alps in December. Nevertheless, he followed the light until he came to a large stone wall where the light disappeared over the top. All at once, he heard a shriek that pierced the silence and chilled him to the core. The hairs on his neck stood upright. At one end of the wall, a figure emerged from the mist. Max couldn't distinguish if it was the silhouette of an animal or a human. It was huge, bigger than any man he had ever seen. Max noticed the shadow had enormous curled horns. Its eyes suddenly lit up in a bright blood red, and the beast shrieked again.

Run! Without thinking, Max sprinted down the length of the stone wall and found a hole that looked large enough for him to squeeze through. It looked like a way to escape, and continuing to run down the length of the wall seemed like a bad idea. When he scurried into the hole, he heard a sound like a door being closed behind him. He turned around quickly to see what happened, but since he could still see the forest through the hole, he paid no mind to it. Max didn't think the beast had followed him, but now the light was nowhere to be seen. As his eyes adjusted to the darkness, he realized he was inside a castle ruin. Max had read stories about castles, but now he was actually standing in one! He wondered if brave knights fought battles here or held jousting events. Still shaking with adrenaline, he snapped back to the moment. *What was that thing?*

"Max," a voice whispered. "Max ... over here." The voice startled him, and he couldn't see anything in the darkness. Emerging from the shadows, a figure began to take shape. A lantern in the figure's hand revealed what appeared to be an old man. He looked frail at first, but upon closer inspection, he didn't look super old, just tired maybe. He was wearing a green-and-brown coat and had a gray beard twice the size of his head. A twisted wooden staff was in his other hand, and a hat interwoven with twigs and berries adorned his head. On his face, through his massive beard, appeared a smile.

"How d..do you know m..my name?" Max said nervously.

"I know every little boy's name, and I know that you want *War of the Planets 2* for Christmas this year," replied the man. "You cannot go back home just yet, Max. The beast has seen you, and he means to steal your sense of wonderment. Follow me to find it." The man turned and walked down a hallway within the stone castle ramparts.

Now, normally, following a strange-looking old man down a dark castle tunnel would be a definite no, a no-brainer, but Max felt at peace and somehow knew he could trust the man. Besides, there was no way he was going back into the forest where that thing was. But how did this man know his name and what he wanted for Christmas? Or why did he even care? Max hadn't yet told his dad or anyone what he wanted.

As he walked into the tunnel, he felt alive. His heart was racing, and his hands were shaking. He put his hand into his pocket to grasp his silver locket. It made him feel safe and not so alone. The cold, damp walls dripped water onto him, and he could smell the humidity in the air. Eventually, he heard noises coming from up ahead and saw a light. The noises grew louder, and he could hear laughing and whispers.

"Welcome!" A small being no bigger than a little child shouted gleefully in a high-pitched voice. Max's eyes adjusted to his surroundings, revealing a small village before him. Tiny wood homes lined a single street through the center of the village, and dozens of small beings were scrambling about. The creature in front of him was wrinkled and a little pudgy for his height. He had a smile, no, a grin, so big and so bright that for a moment, Max almost caught himself smiling back. Max thought he must be dreaming. *This can't be right. Maybe I hit my head on the wall, or there was some sort of sleep agent in the hot cocoa I drank.* Whatever it was, he had never seen or been to a place like this before.

"Welcome to Santa's village!" the little creature cried out joyfully, practically jumping up and down.

Max turned around in shock to look at the old man. He wasn't fat, didn't have a white beard and wasn't wearing a red suit. But his smile confirmed his identity without him saying a word.

"I've been waiting for you," the man said.

Still in shock, Max shouted, "NO WAY! I can't believe you're real!"

"Oh I'm real," he said, "but not for everyone. Come, let's get you warmed up."

Chapter 5:
The Weihnachtsmann and the Woodlings

Max continued to stare at Santa in disbelief as they walked up a small hill and past dozens more small beings with beady eyes. They stared at Max in careful curiosity.

Max wondered aloud, "Are they ... uh ...?"

"Elves?" Santa interrupted. "No, they aren't elves. They're called Wichtel, or as I call them, Woodlings. They are the key to my toy production and essential to my fight against Krampus." They weren't the brightly colored, pointy-hat-wearing elves Max had pictured in his mind. In fact, they appeared quite dull and drab, with gray and brown clothing. They came in all shapes and sizes: skinny ones, fat ones, hairy ones, short ones. With the exception of the first one who greeted him, they had one thing in common.

"How come some of them look so sad?" Max asked.

"They are afraid," Santa said, shaking his head.

"Afraid of what?"

Santa was silent. At the top of the hill, they entered a small cabin with a roaring fireplace, and Max took a seat by the fire. His head was spinning, and the reality of the situation seemed too much to comprehend.

"Here," Santa said as he wrapped a soft, fuzzy blanket around Max.

Max's teeth were chattering. He was shaking, probably more out of being in shock than being cold. Still, he managed to ask, "Who is Krampus?"

Santa sat silently as if lost in thought and then answered, "He is Knecht Ruprect, the beast you saw at the castle wall." Santa paused for a moment. "A war is raging, Max, and I need your help."

"A war? What are you talking about? You're supposed to be all about toys and reindeer and stuff. Happy things. And besides, don't you live at the North Pole?" Max asked inquisitively.

"No, no, don't be silly. The North Pole is much too cold," Santa exclaimed.

"There's nothing there but ice! I'll tell you all about it later. Right now, all is not well in my village, Max. Little boys and girls don't want to play with toys anymore. Christmas lists are getting shorter and shorter each year. Krampus knows this and has made it his mission to destroy all of Christmas ... and the Woodlings and me along with it."

"Why does Krampus want to destroy Christmas?"

"Well you see, Max," Santa explained as he sat forward in his chair, "he used to work for me, many, many moons ago. It was his job to punish and scare children in this area who misbehaved and landed on my naughty list. It was meant to be a small fright, like hitting them with a bundle of sticks, a sharp nasty sting and just enough for them to be good again and get them back on the nice list. Even good kids do bad things sometimes, but I think everyone deserves a second chance, don't you, Max?" Santa peered at him.

"Uh yeah, I guess so," Max replied, looking down. He could think of many times when he wasn't so good this year. He didn't even know which list his name would be on.

Santa continued, "But the more the years went on, and the more Krampus dealt out punishments, the more he changed into something evil and twisted. He began to …" Santa looked at Max again, this time with a twisted face.

"What?" Max whispered, sitting straight up in his chair. He waited, knowing whatever it was wasn't good.

"He began to eat the children," Santa said in a clear, low voice. Max shivered. He knew he heard him right but still couldn't believe it.

"It has gone unnoticed by society because Krampus has been smart not to bring too much attention to the situation by stretching this out over several years and at places all over the region.

Despite the look on Max's face, Santa continued. "I had to banish him from my village, and ever since then, he has sworn vengeance against me. His power appears to grow every time a child loses his or her sense of joy and wonderment for Christmas or when a child is taken away to his lair. Max, you are the first child I've allowed to see me, and do you know why?"

"Why?" asked Max.

"I need a child who doesn't believe in me and has lost his Christmas spirit so that child can believe again. I need you to help me come up with an idea for the best Christmas toy ever."

Chapter 6:
Dreams of Christmas Past

"But I don't even play with toys anymore," Max said.

"I know," Santa said, shaking his head sadly. "But that's precisely why I need you. What if you wanted to play with something again? Something you wanted more than anything else in the world?" Santa asked optimistically.

Max didn't say anything, so Santa continued, "Krampus grows stronger every day, and I'm running out of time. I fear the Woodlings can't take much more. A new toy that every child wants would weaken him and return the Christmas spirit to the world. Do you know what Christmas spirit is, Max?"

"I guess I haven't really thought about it. I was little the last time Christmas meant anything in my family," Max said.

"Well," Santa said, standing, "my hope is that you'll soon find out. But enough for now; you need your rest. We'll discuss this in the morning."

"But, I have to get back to my dad! He'll worry."

"I understand your concern about your dad, but it's not safe with Krampus and his Darklings lurking in the forest. He may suspect you're with me, and although he can't find my village, he is lord of the dark woods that surround us. Rest for now; we'll talk more in the morning."

Santa sprinkled something into a mug full of hot chocolate and handed it to Max. He led Max outside to a one-room cabin with a soft-looking bed and a fireplace that crackled in the corner. Out of habit, Max's eyes quickly scanned for a TV, but there was none. Santa left him alone, and Max sat on the edge of the bed, staring at the fire. He started to think about the day's events. *How did I get into this mess? Is my dad okay?* Max could not believe Santa was real! As he stared into the fire, a shape began to take form. Max sat up a bit. Horns curled from the flames, and glowing eyes danced in the light. In that moment, Max knew Krampus was also real. He shook his head, and the image in the fire went away, but Max was still worried. He knew he would have nightmares that night. He sipped on the cocoa, and a tingling feeling came over him. His fears instantly subsided. Exhausted, he was soon fast asleep.

That night, instead of a nightmare, Max dreamt about the first Christmas he could remember. He must have been four or five. The dream was exactly how it really happened except that in the morning when he and his parents gathered around the tree to open presents, there weren't any. His parents looked surprised and sad. Just then, they disappeared in a cloud of white-blue smoke, and a noise emanated from the chimney. Max noticed one black boot appeared, then a second. Before he knew it, Santa was standing in front of him. He was adorned in his traditional red suit, white beard encircling his round face, and his belly bounced like a bowl full of jelly. Santa didn't say a word but held out his hand to give Max a present. Max was filled with joy. He tore off the wrapping paper and opened the gift. A smile appeared on his face as he gazed down at the present. What was it?

Chapter 7:

A Cabin in the Snow

Before the dream could reveal Santa's present, Max suddenly woke up. He was freezing! The fire had died out in the middle of the night, and the room felt like an icebox. He looked around for some wood but couldn't find any. Then he saw a note near the fireplace. It read, "Wood is outside on the back side of the cabin." *Really?* Max thought. *They can't keep a stock of wood inside?* Max had been cold before but never this bone-chilling kind of cold. He certainly didn't want to go outside where it was even colder. Then another thought came to him. *Where is the bathroom?* There was just one room in the little cabin, so he figured it must be outside as well. After several minutes of dreading getting out of his bed, he yelled out in frustration, "Fine!" and he stomped to the door, opening it carefully. He looked around, but there was only silence and the moonlight shining down on the snow.

"Help!" Max shouted but not too loud. No answer.

"Um, hello?" still no reply. He closed the cabin door and got back under the blanket in bed. After a few minutes, he realized it was no use: he had to go to the bathroom. Besides, it was too cold to sleep. He would have to get the wood himself. He grabbed his coat, slipped on his boots and walked through the crunchy snow around to the back of the cabin. For a moment, he thought he saw something, but it was only his shadow on the snow from the moonlight. Then some birds flew overhead and caught his attention. They flew in a funny kind of way, and it only took a couple of minutes for Max to realize they weren't birds. They were bats. Max liked bats, but under these circumstances, when he was all alone in the cold night in a place he didn't know, it was one more reason to quicken his step. A small wooden shack was a few yards from the cabin. Max decided he needed to take a look inside. It *was* the bathroom, if you could call it that! It was just a hole in the ground with a very cold toilet seat on top of a wooden box. Max went to the bathroom as fast as he could. Around the other side of the cabin was the woodpile. The logs were cold, and he had to brush snow off the top of the pile first. He returned to his cabin with a few pieces of wood and threw them on the floor. He was much colder now and desperate to get the fire going again. When he put a couple of the pieces in the fireplace, nothing happened. They didn't catch fire.

Now what? he thought. If only he had signed up for Boy Scouts back in Virginia like his dad wanted him to. Looking around the cabin, he was able to find a few scraps of paper but not much else. He only had one shot at this. One of the scraps of paper caught fire from the embers but quickly extinguished next to one of the larger logs. Maybe if he used what little paper he had to catch a smaller stick on fire and then used that stick to catch one of the larger logs on fire …

It worked! Gradually, the fire started to spread to the other logs, and before he knew it, he had a roaring fire. Satisfied with his accomplishment, he crawled back in bed and quickly fell asleep again.

Chapter 8:

Santa's Reindeer

Max awoke in the morning and looked around the quiet room. The fire's smoldering embers were glowing, keeping the room warm. He was surprised to find he was still in Santa's village. That part wasn't a dream. Gazing out of the window, he could see the sun's light reflecting off newly fallen snow clinging to every branch of the trees nearby. The silence of the morning was so peaceful.

"Guten morgen!" a small Woodling said, breaking the silence.

"Good morning," Max replied, figuring that the Woodling's words in German sounded so much like good morning that he had to be right.

"My name is Moritz. Santa has asked you to join him in the stables, just down the hill." Moritz was the same Woodling who first greeted Max when he entered the village. He was a stout, hairy little guy with a very welcoming face. He seemed much more cheerful than the other Woodlings. Max liked him immediately.

"Can you really help us?" Moritz asked.

"I don't know," Max replied. "I'm just a kid."

"Well if Santa chose you, then you're really special."

"I'm not special," Max quickly responded. "I don't even know what I'm doing here."

"Don't worry, Santa knows," replied Moritz with a slight grin. "There are some clothes that should fit you in those drawers over in the corner." Max wondered how there were children's clothes in the drawers, but he needed a change and didn't give it a second thought. He put on the boots and trudged through the snow to the stables. The Woodlings' huts and nearby trees were plain and not decorated in a way that screamed "Santa's elf village." They were a stark contrast to the Christmas market in Dinkelstadt from the night before. Here, an enormous Christmas tree stood in the center of the village, but it didn't have any ornaments or lights on it. In fact, the whole scene seemed pretty drab and dreary.

Max got to what he assumed were the horse stables and found Santa inside feeding carrots to real reindeer! They sort of looked like regular deer, except they had silver-like fur and bigger antlers.

"Max, thank you for joining me on this fine morning. Would you grab a bucket and help out?"

"Do they fly and pull your sleigh?" Max asked, picking up a bucket.

"Of course, they do!" laughed Santa. Then in a more serious tone, he said, "Although I worry there isn't enough Christmas magic for them to fly for very long. Here, take this bunch of Brussels sprouts over to Gassy, won't you?"

"Gassy?" Max replied. "Isn't it Dancer and Prancer, Donder, Blitzen, and so on?"

"No, those were made-up names in a book about Christmas a long time ago. This is Gassy; he doesn't eat carrots or hay but loves

Brussels sprouts. Unfortunately, they make him fart like crazy. Needless to say, Gassy goes up in front of the sleigh team rather than closer to the back where the sleigh is." Santa continued, "That's No Horns. Obviously, she doesn't have any horns. Over there is Gramps, the oldest reindeer in the land; twelve years old and still going strong. Three Hooves is missing a leg, but she still flies with the best of them. Then there's Crabby. He is always in a bad mood and will kick you in the gut if you get too close to him. Humbo and Bumbo here are brothers and are the largest reindeer in existence. And last but not least, Bambi," Santa finished.

"I see why you named the other reindeer what you named them, but why Bambi?"

"I just loved that movie," Santa said.

"No Rudolph?" Max inquired.

"No, the idea of a reindeer with a red nose that lights up is just silly, don't you think?" asked Santa.

"I guess so," said Max as he put the pail up to Gassy's muzzle, and the reindeer quickly turned away.

"Like this, with a flat hand," said Santa. Gassy began munching out of Max's hand, and Max thought of the toxic gas cloud that would soon be upon them.

"Where did they come from?" inquired Max.

"Mostly from Sweden and Norway. Hey, don't step in the …" As soon as Max heard the wet, squishing sound, he knew what he had stepped in. Reindeer poop. A huge pile too.

"Aww gross!" Max exclaimed.

"There is a water well with a pump over on the side of the barn. Here, let me show you where," Santa said. The pungent odor was now burning his nose hairs. As Max began washing off the bottom of his shoes, Santa spoke again.

"Do you know what tonight is, Max?" But before he could reply, Santa continued. "Tonight is Krampusnacht, December 5. It's the night when Krampus and his legion of Perchten, or as I call them, Darklings, go out in search of children. They punish, frighten, and steal the children. It is also the only night that I know where he will be." Max's face suddenly changed to that of concern and fear.

"Don't worry, Max, you're safe here with me."

Santa's reassurance comforted Max, but he wished Santa hadn't told him what Krampusnacht was and especially that it was tonight.

Chapter 9:

A Call to Action

After the feeding and washing off, they walked into the small Woodling village and entered a grand, wooden, temple-like house. Long tables filled the room, with rows of Woodlings eating in a most raucous way.

"My friends," Santa shouted, and the noise quickly died down. "THIS is Max. He will be dining with us today." Some grumblings and some cheers could be heard as they sat down at one of the tables. A big bowl of some sort of brown stew was passed in front of Max.

"Goulash!" yelled Moritz, seated next to Max. "Try it, Max! Otto makes the best goulash." It sounded awful, and it didn't look much better, like it was either made of goo or something a ghoul would eat. The Woodlings were slurping it down so loudly and making such a mess that Max almost lost his appetite. As if snapping at his dad, he blurted out, "I don't want that."

The conversation and chatter quickly went quiet, and the Woodlings stared at him in a confused manner. Max immediately wished he had put his foot in his mouth.

"I mean, sure, I'll give it a try." He hadn't eaten anything other than his own fingernails since the Christmas market with his dad, and his grumbling stomach soon won out. Surprisingly, the smell was intoxicating, and the taste was delicious. He quickly found he was slurping it down alongside the Woodlings.

Throughout the course of the meal, the Woodlings just stared at Max off and on.

"Do you have a special power? Can you defeat Krampus?" a couple of them asked. Moritz had left by then, and Max found himself wishing he had a friendly and familiar face at the table. He couldn't believe that these were Santa's toymakers. All the stories he had read or heard about Santa's elves suddenly seemed greatly exaggerated. In fact, nothing was like what he expected, not the Woodlings, the reindeer, Krampus or even Santa.

"I hope you saved room for the stollen," Santa said. It was a fruit bread covered in powdered sugar and was every bit as delicious as everything had been that evening. Max was used to a diet of chicken nuggets and soda and had never really eaten *real* food.

"Have you thought about my request, Max?" Santa spoke up.

"You mean for a toy?" Max replied. "I ... I had a dream that I was opening a present under the Christmas tree, but I couldn't see what the present was. I'm still not sure what to make of all this."

"Keep dreaming, Max. It will come to you."

"Santa! Santa!" exclaimed Moritz as he burst into the dining hall. "It's Jannik. He's wandered off beyond the wall! And on Krampusnacht! Santa, you have to do something! We HAVE to save him!" he begged.

"What does that mean?" asked Max aloud.

"It means he'll likely be captured or killed," one of the Woodlings responded woefully.

"Yes of course, Moritz, we will leave at once," said Santa. "I need volunteers." The Woodlings were scared, scared of Krampus and Krampusnacht. No one stepped forward, and the look of disbelief in Moritz's eyes saddened Max in a way he hadn't expected. *Is the Woodling society really this broken?*

"I'll help," Max finally said.

"Are you sure, Max? It will be quite dangerous," Santa replied.

"Yes, I'm sure," he said, but his mind was trying to catch up to his words and comprehend what he had just agreed to. His mom had always taught him to help those in need, and he often found himself agreeing to things he didn't want to do. It didn't matter anyway; there was no turning back now.

"Are we going to take out your sleigh?" Max asked, a little excited at that thought.

"No, I only take the reindeer out on Christmas Eve. It's too risky to endanger the reindeer on Krampusnacht when Krampus and his Darklings are at their most powerful."

That made sense, but Max couldn't help feeling disappointed, and the thought of all that walking in the cold wasn't sounding appealing either. They gathered food and supplies and put on warmer coats, then the three set out on foot through a dark tunnel lit only by lanterns.

Chapter 10:
Darklings

At the end of the tunnel was a huge thicket of ivy.

"Why would a Woodling wander out beyond the wall?" Max asked.

"Many Woodlings have left my village over the last several years," Santa explained. "Some have lost hope and faith, and others believe it is only a matter of time until ..." Santa stopped midsentence. They felt their way through the twisting vines. On the other side was a large, circular wooden door with big symbols carved into it.

"They are runes," Santa said as he pulled a large iron lever on the side, and the door slowly opened.

"What do they mean?" Max wondered aloud.

Santa replied, "It says, 'A child's soul is the heart of Christmas.'" The phrase was a relief to him as he was expecting it to be a warning of certain death or something.'" The symbols looked familiar to him. *Where have I seen them? My locket!* He pulled the locket out of his pocket and inspected it closely. Sure enough, some of the symbols were the same! *What does it all mean?* Max was about to ask Santa about the meaning of the symbols on his locket when Santa interrupted.

"Let's get moving while there is still light left." On the other side of the door, the snow was coming down hard, and Max could see the dark foreboding forest in front of him. He was suddenly filled with dread. An icy shiver ran through his body as he flashed back to his first encounter with Krampus.

"Can't we take one of these lanterns?" he asked.

"No, it will reveal our position to the Darklings or the Nachtkrapp," replied Santa. "Don't worry, young Max, I know the way." The words comforted him somewhat, but he was terrified just the same.

"What the heck are Nachtkrapp?" Max asked.

"They are nocturnal raven-like creatures with human arms that do the bidding of Krampus. They most likely won't harm you if you are in a group, but they would certainly give our position away," Santa said. Snowstorm, Darklings, Nachtkrapp and the possibility of a Krampus appearance at any second? How he suddenly longed for the lonely boredom of life in his dad's apartment playing video games. At least there, he would be safe and warm.

The three walked through the snowy woods for a while. The whole time, Max was sure Krampus was going to jump out from behind a tree at any moment and spill Max's guts on the forest floor. As his eyes adjusted to the darkness, his mind began playing tricks on him. The wind was howling, and shapes were forming and then disappearing as he kept trying to see through the thick snow flying in his face and stinging like needles. He hadn't expected to encounter a winter storm and was severely underdressed.

"How much longer, Santa?" he whined.

"We're almost there, Max. Hang in there!" Santa yelled over the noise of the storm. The wind and the fear finally dissipated a bit when they came to the edge of town. The Christmas market was now closed, and the village was eerily quiet. Back in civilization again, Max thought of his dad and how he was probably worried sick over Max's whereabouts. He struggled to stay focused on the task at hand. Even if he didn't fully understand why it was so important, he felt compelled to help Moritz find Jannik. Maybe all that time spent cooped up in his dad's apartment had caused him to crave real-life adventures, experiences he thought could only be played out with a controller in his hands. Maybe he subconsciously saw it as a way to get back to his dad. It was certainly exciting, and his mind was racing to understand when Santa spoke up and broke the silence.

"Any sign of Jannik?" he asked. "Nothing yet," replied Moritz.

"W..w..what exactly are D..D..Darklings?" Max asked, his teeth chattering.

"You'll find out soon ... there goes one," Santa said, pointing. "See? It's heading into that house on the corner."

Max saw the dark figure. The Darkling slithered up to the door of a half-timbered house. It was almost dark out, but Max could make out the shape of the creature, short and skinny and without a single hair on its head. Although scary, cold and gray-looking, something was familiar about them.

Chapter 11:

Terror at the Krampuslauf

"We need to try and help the child who lives in that house. Stand still, Max. We are about to enter the house by way of transfusion." Santa pulled out his staff, lifting it over his head. A blue light enveloped the group, and instantaneously, they were inside the house in the upstairs room.

"Epic!" Max exclaimed, "How did you d..do that?"

"Christmas magic, of course. It only works in distances of fifty yards or less, though."

"C..can you do it any t..time you w..want?"

"Shhh," Santa whispered, "the Darkling will hear you." At that very moment, Max could hear the steps creaking as the thing climbed the staircase. A young boy was sleeping in his bed not more than seven feet away from them. They stood in the corner of the room as the bedroom door slowly opened. At first, the Darkling couldn't see them as it crept toward the bed. Then Max's teeth began chattering again, breaking the silence.

"Be gone, foul creature," Santa exclaimed suddenly and forcefully. The thing turned at the group in shock and shrieked loudly. Max suddenly saw the fear in its eyes. As the boy in bed awoke, the Darkling ran out of the room and down the stairs. Santa quickly used transfusion to get the group back to the street in town. They could still hear the creature screeching as if to alarm other nearby Darklings.

"We must move quickly; they know we are here now," Santa commanded. A noise coming from around the corner seemed to get louder and louder. They heard music and clanging bells, and a crowd of people came into view. Following the crowd was Krampus! Then another Krampus? And another? Dozens of Krampuses carrying torches taunted the crowd and hit people with sticks. Bells clanged through the streets. *What is going on?*

"It's a Krampuslauf," Santa explained. "Krampus has a cult following of people who like to dress up like him on Krampusnacht and scare people. They even have someone dress up like me and follow the Krampuses through town."

"Why w..would they d..do that? D..don't they k..know that Krampus is evil?"

"Some people just like to be scared and don't necessarily think Krampus exists for real. Others are simply following an age-old tradition in the folklore of this area. This may work to our advantage, as we can move about town easier without being noticed."

They moved toward a narrow back street and then several streets over, away from the crowds. Then at the end of the street and through the falling snow, Moritz spotted Jannik.

"Brother!" he yelled and began running down the street toward him.

"Moritz! Stop!" cried Santa. Suddenly, the beast Krampus, the *real* Krampus, appeared out of nowhere and grabbed Moritz, placing him under his arm at his side. He gazed at Santa and Max and let out a ghastly snarl. Then with Moritz still in his clutches, he began stomping his way up the street toward them, and Max noticed that he had a hoof on one of his legs where there should have been a foot! Krampus was no more than twenty feet away with his nostrils flared and blowing steam into the night air.

"Santa, help!" Max yelled. Santa raised his staff, and a blue light shot out of it, creating a wall of blue light in front of them. Krampus halted his approach. He snorted loudly and shrieked an awful noise, then turned and ran down the street. Moritz was still in the clutches of Krampus, and Max could see the terror in his eyes.

"He's gone!" cried Jannik. "My brother is gone, and it's all my fault!"

"Come, Jannik, we must get back to the village or risk getting taken ourselves," Santa said. He reminded Max that Krampus's power was at its peak on Krampusnacht and that Santa had no way of knowing where the beast had gone.

"We have to hope that Moritz is still alive and that an opportunity to save him will present itself soon," explained Santa.

"C..can't you use y…your m..magic to save him? You're S..Santa!" Max exclaimed. Santa replied with a sad face. "Alas, young Max, my power is not what it once was." His forlorn look surprised Max as he turned away.

Chapter 12:

Buried Alive

The cold was really getting to Max now, and he couldn't feel his feet.

"Santa? I think Max needs help," urged Jannik. Santa grabbed Max's hands, and his eyes got big as a look of concern washed over his face. Max was worried now.

"Quickly! We must find shelter!" yelled Santa. They raced into the woods and began searching for some sort of relief from the storm. They found a grouping of large boulders that looked like their best chance. Santa and Jannik began feverishly digging snow and dirt out from under several rocks. Eventually, they created a small opening to crawl into that led to an open space created by a few large boulders.

"Jannik, gather what little firewood you can. We have to get Max warmed up."

"But Santa, it will give away our position!"

"We don't have a choice, Jannik. He may lose his fingers and toes if we don't act now!" Max was feeling sleepy all of a sudden, and the cold numbness was seeping into his chest. In the corner of the carved-out shelter, they started a small fire and lay beside it for hours as the storm raged outside.

"This is my fault," said Santa. "It was foolish of me to bring you with me. Try to stay awake, Max. Think warm thoughts."

"Am I g...going to have to have m...my fingers ch..chopped off?" Max asked, frightened of what answer he might receive.

"Let me see your hands, Max," said Santa. He looked at them and showed them to Jannik, mumbling something that Max couldn't understand.

"I don't like the looks of this one," Santa spoke up. "I give it twenty more minutes. If we don't see any improvement, I think it needs to come off." When Max heard this, he fainted.

He must have been out for several hours because water droplets were falling on his forehead when he finally woke up. The sun's rays were shining through crevices in the rocks, and water was dripping all around them. His fingers. He quickly lifted his hands to check. 1 2 3 4 5 6 7 8 9 10–all there. He was relieved for sure but somehow felt as though something else was missing. He reached into his pocket for his locket. Gone. He frantically searched his other pockets, but it was still missing. An intense sadness washed over him. *How could I have lost the one thing I had left from Mom? Maybe it is back at my cabin*, he thought. There was little time to dwell on this because Max realized they had other issues to contend with. They were buried! Jannik had already been at it for hours, digging toward the surface, but had made little headway. They all took turns digging in the tunnel, and it went on for several more hours. At least he was warm now. They finally reached the top only to begin the long walk back to the village. Without snowshoes, it was slow and filled with sadness. No one spoke a word, and Jannik sobbed the entire way.

"It's always this way on Krampusnacht," said Jannik as they walked behind Santa. "Everyone is terrified that this will be Santa's last Christmas."

"Why would it be his last Christmas?" Max asked.

"His power has become weak because the children no longer believe in him or play with toys. And now Moritz is gone. What cruel fate awaits us next!" Max had to think of a toy that would help Santa. But he couldn't think of anything. *Virtual reality? A new game system? A drone? No, nothing like that.* Maybe it would come to him in his sleep. If he could sleep at all, that is. Max would be haunted by another encounter with Krampus, charging toward the group with glowing red eyes.

Chapter 13:
The Lutzelfrau

"There is a place up ahead where we have to make a stop," Santa spoke up. The group came over a small hill in a dark part of the forest, and Max could see smoke coming from the chimney of what appeared to be a small round hut made of sticks.

"Who lives there?" Max questioned.

"She is the Lutzelfrau, the Yule witch," said Santa. Max gave Jannik a questioning look, but Jannik shrugged his shoulders as if to say, "I don't know what Santa is talking about."

"The Lutzelfrau isn't your typical witch. She isn't necessarily a bad witch or a good witch, but she knows a lot about this forest as well as Krampus, and it is said that she is able to see things past, present and future. She needs a small gift from us, or she won't speak to us. Max, do you have any fruit or gingerbread left?"

"A little bit," Max replied, digging in his pocket.

"It's not much, but it will have to do," said Santa. They approached the hut, and Max could hear what sounded like a low-toned haunting chant coming from inside. He was biting his nails again and noticed that they were nearly worn down to the nub. When he was younger, his parents read Grimm fairy tales to him; the tale of Hansel and Gretel had always terrified him. *Witches in the forest are here to fatten up and eat children, not help them*, he thought. And here he was, in the same area where Grimm fairy tales took place, in a dark forest … about to encounter a real witch. If he stopped to dwell on this fact, he would chicken out in a second, so he tried his best to block it from his mind. Several cats were lounging around the entrance, and an odd smell of sharp spices hung in the air.

"Who's there?" the Lutzelfrau stopped chanting and spoke out with a frightened tone.

"It's the Weihnachtsmann," replied Santa.

"What Christmas presents have you brought for me?" she asked.

"Lebkuchen gingerbread," replied Santa. There was some banging and clanging of what sounded like pots and pans. Then a soft white hand appeared and slowly pulled a piece of cloth to one side, revealing a small circular entrance to the hut. The witch! Santa entered the hut, and before Max knew it, he was walking toward the entrance too. It's like his feet had a mind of their own and were taking him to places he had never dreamed he would go. He looked back at Jannik, who was stone-petrified with fear and shaking his head no.

The first thing Max noticed upon entering were cracks of light breaking into the darkness from rips in the canvas roof. All sorts of things you would expect to see in a witch's hut were hanging everywhere from the ceiling. Sticks, animal skulls, feathers, bowls and pots were strewn all over the tables as if the place had never been cleaned. As Max's eyes adjusted to the dark, he caught his first glimpse of the witch. What he expected to see and what he actually saw were entirely different. Even though her clothes were rags and her hair was all frizzy, she was pretty in a plain sort of way and was smiling at them!

"Season's blessings to you! Welcome," she spoke in a friendly tone. "Do you have the gingerbread?" she inquired. Santa handed her the gingerbread, and her smile turned to a frown.

"This is not nearly enough!" she said angrily.

"Please taste it before you make any judgment," Santa replied quickly. She gave a skeptical look but then took a bite. The smile was back. Max was beginning to see what Santa meant by not exactly a good witch and not exactly a bad witch.

"What is it that you need, Weihnachtsmann?"

"I need to see the future."

"Very well, we will see what we see." She rooted through sacks and boxes, looking for things. Then she started placing items in a bowl. Pine needles, a plant that looked like it could be mistletoe, a rose petal. Then she went over to Santa, plucked a hair from his gray beard and added that to the mix. She poured hot water into the bowl and began to stare at it. After a couple of minutes waiting in silence, she spoke up.

"I see a woman."

"Yes?" Santa said eagerly.

"She is alive, but she is in grave danger! She is someplace dark. A basement maybe? No, a cave, most definitely a cave."

"What does it mean? What else do you see?"

"The vision is fading. She is about to …"

"About to what?" Santa pressed.

"About to … I'm sorry, it's gone." Santa's face had the look of disappointment and confusion at the same time.

"Was this the past, present or future?" Santa asked the witch.

"Hard to tell. I'm sorry, I wish I had more. You may leave through the door you came in."

"Could you answer a couple more questions for me?" Santa asked.

"Do you have more gingerbread?" asked the witch.

"No, I'm sorry, I don't. But I have something else. Max? Can you wait outside for a minute?" Max had a puzzled look on his face but did as Santa wished and left the hut.

Max and Jannik waited around for a little while. Max pondered what Santa was asking the witch or what else he had given her. He could hear them talking to one another but couldn't hear well enough to understand what the conversation was about. Santa emerged from the hut and said they were leaving.

"I hope you got the answers you were looking for Weihnachtsmann." shouted the witch. "Come back any time, but bring more of that gingerbread!"

Chapter 14: The Naughty List

As their trek back continued, Max thought about asking Santa what the Yule witch had seen in the bowl. *What woman was in grave danger?* Max was too nervous to ask about it, though, and he thought that if Santa wanted to talk about it, he would have. After an hour or so, they were finally back in the village. An exhausted Max entered his cabin and quickly began looking for the locket. After several minutes, he realized it was hopeless and got into bed. He kept thinking about the missing locket, their encounter with the Lutzelfrau Yule witch, and the look of terror on Moritz's face as he was being carried away by Krampus. He remembered everything about the Darkling he saw too. It was gray, skeletal and stealthy. Max again thought something was familiar about the creature. But he still couldn't quite figure out what it was. His thoughts wouldn't keep him up, though; he was too tired and fell quickly asleep.

The next day, Santa was busy working on ideas to help save Moritz. The Woodlings scrambled around, working at a feverish pace on what Max assumed were toys and digging themselves out of all the snow. Santa had told Max that he could write a letter to his dad to relieve his dad's worry about Max's whereabouts. Even though Max was sure his father wouldn't believe the letter, he wrote,

"Hi Dad, I'm helping Santa Claus defeat the evil lord Krampus and save Christmas. Be back soon. Signed, Max." Yeah, sure, *that* was believable. So instead, he decided the truth was too confusing and would only complicate matters if he ever made it home. He walked over to tell Santa that he wouldn't be sending his dad a letter and found him sitting on the porch of his cabin, reading letters and smoking a pipe. Dark-rimmed reading glasses were framed by the lines on his face, and the smell of tobacco and cherries hung in the air from the smoke.

"Hi, Santa."

"Good evening, Max. Do you have a letter to your father you want me to send? Will he be glad to hear from you?"

"I don't think I'm gonna send one," Max replied. "He wouldn't believe me, plus he's never around anyways. He probably doesn't even know that I'm gone."

"You aren't always around either, though, are you?" Santa responded. Max thought about it for a second and realized Santa was probably right. He was always online with friends and his dad was always working in his office. But even though they hadn't seen much of each other recently, Max missed his dad a lot.

"A father's love is a wonderful gift. If our mission succeeds, you will hopefully receive a great deal more of it." Max didn't understand what Santa meant. Santa's words sometimes had a way of sounding like a riddle.

"Are those other letters to you from kids?"

"Oh these?" he replied, holding up the papers. "This is the naughty list."

"Um, am I on there?" Max asked in a timid voice, his mind racing to think of all the bad behavior he had committed over the years.

"What do you think?" replied Santa through mild laughter. "But don't worry, Max. I'm sure you've already done more than enough to stay off of my list this year." It was good to see Santa in a positive mood.

"Most children are good and innocent by nature. They may behave badly or make mistakes from time to time, but they can always make up for that with good behavior the closer it gets to Christmas. Come with me, Max. I want to show you the Woodlings' workshops."

Chapter 15:

Making Toys

Further down the hill, they came upon rows of large wooden cabins.

"The Woodlings have been with me for centuries," Santa began. "In fact, I can't remember a time they weren't around. Legend has it that humans and Woodlings lived together peacefully in this area at one time, and there were even cities full of thousands of them. But somewhere along the way, they were pushed into smaller and smaller groups. Even here in my village, more than two hundred once lived here. Now we are down to thirty-seven. They are the last of their kind and could be destined for extinction. They work for me because they are creatures born of true Christmas spirit. It is all they know, and I am grateful for their help. Some of them can even speak up to 6,500 known world languages. I warn you, however, they are extremely superstitious as well as notorious pranksters."

"This first cabin is the wooden toy department." Santa opened the door, and Max saw a few Woodlings working with power saws, wood lathes, band saws, belt sanders and other tools.

"This used to be our largest department," Santa said. "But alas, well, you know the story." It certainly didn't remind Max of images of elves with pointy green hats working on wooden toys in a clean, brightly colored room. Rather, it was pretty musty and drab, with sawdust all over the floor. The next cabin featured assorted dolls, such as Barbies, American Girls and babies. This cabin was a little busier but still pretty messy. They walked down the path further still, and Santa showed Max the cabins with all of the toy guns, trains, cars, action figures, stuffed animals and robots. Max thought maybe Santa was showing them to him to help spark an idea, but he didn't see how this would help. Of course, Santa could be showing him around for no other reason than to familiarize Max with the Woodlings and their culture. Next was not a toy workshop but something that looked like a chemistry lab out of the movie *Frankenstein*.

"This is our potion apothecary," said Santa, and this is Frauka, our alchemist. She helps me with various potions and spells to make up for my weakening Christmas magic."

"A pleasure to meet you, Max," said Frauka. She was taller than most of the Woodlings and had stringy hair that gave her a very plain look overall. But she seemed friendly enough, and Max was more than curious about all the spells and concoctions she was capable of creating. The place was a mess with tons of books, bottles, beakers and tubes. It kind of had that Yoda's-hut-in-the-swamp feel to it.

"Do you know anything about chemistry, Max?" she asked.

"No, I'm sorry, I don't." He didn't feel too bad about it, though, because he hadn't studied any chemistry at school yet.

"Not to worry. You will soon enough," she said as Santa led Max out of the room. They walked further still down the hill. The last cabin was the smallest. It was the size of a small house, not a toy factory. When Santa opened the door, there was Jannik, sitting at a computer! It was the first piece of electronics Max had seen in some time, and he wondered how they got the power for it. Especially considering they didn't even have running water. Jannik was petting a small animal of some sort.

"What is that?" Max asked Jannik curiously.

"It's Moritz's pet hedgehog. He would want me to take care of it for him. He's not a wild hedgehog, so he doesn't need to hibernate in the winter."

It was the cutest little creature with hundreds of tiny spikes all over its back, making it look like a baby porcupine. *Now, if every kid can get one of these for Christmas instead of a toy,* Max thought, *Krampus won't stand a chance.*

"What's that you're feeding him?" Max inquired.

"He likes slugs," replied Jannik. "Moritz would always feed him slugs. The only hard part is finding 'em in winter."

"This is our computer and video game department," Santa interrupted. "It is comprised of only Jannik and Moritz. Well, now only Jannik," he said under his breath.

"But why is the computer and game department your smallest department?" Max asked. "Kids love computer stuff!" As soon as the words left his mouth, Max understood. Santa nodded.

"Yes, if the computer and game department were any bigger, it would only feed the fire of our own destruction."

"So why even have the department at all?"

Santa continued, "It is my hope that they will come up with

an idea for a game that every kid will want. Remember, that's why you're here, too, Max."

The pressure was mounting for Max, but he couldn't think of anything that hadn't already been done.

"I can't think of anything, Santa."

"Don't concern yourself at this time. It will come to you, Max, I am sure of it." Santa nodded his head in complete belief.

Chapter 16:

A Technological Solution

Santa left the small cabin, and Max spoke to Jannik. Even though Max was only eleven, he knew a fair amount about computers. Not as much as Jannik, who was a genius.

"Take a look at this, Max. It's a 3D printer. The workforce of skilled Woodlings has diminished over the years. Reluctantly, I'm working on designing 3D printers that we can use in various workshops to produce toys twice as fast as we do now." Max watched as one of the machines began creating something, and Jannik started explaining the process. Max didn't understand half of what Jannik was telling him. And he got the feeling that Jannik didn't understand why Santa had put so much faith in Max. It felt strange to think of kids getting toys made by this machine rather than by an elf, er ... Woodling, that is. But it seemed that desperate times called for desperate measures, and they wouldn't be able to keep up with toy production without them. They brainstormed for a while, but he and Jannik just couldn't come up with any ideas. Max didn't see much hope. It was late, and he decided that since they had hit a roadblock, they should call it quits for the evening and try again tomorrow.

The next day, Max woke up thinking about Moritz and his dad and his mom. He wished he could do more to help. He started to feel anxious, but the scent of fresh-baked bread wafting through the windows calmed him. He decided to distract himself by visiting Greta in the bakery. Greta was a Woodling and the head baker. Every morning, she would wake up at the crack of dawn and start baking bread, pretzels, brotchen, pastries and all sorts of delicious treats. She was truly a master at her craft. Max had never been much of an early riser, but somehow, being up before everyone else in the village created a sense of peace within him. Plus, he found the smell of fresh bread quite addictive. All the Woodlings looked forward to the bread and pretzels each day at breakfast and every night at dinner.

At dinner that evening, Max passed out brotchen rolls to the rest of the table and then took his seat next to Jannik. FAARRRT! The Woodlings erupted in laughter. Max had sat on a whoopee cushion, and his face immediately turned red with embarrassment.

"Alright you guys, leave him alone," one of them spoke up quickly. "He's not going to want to help Greta make us this delicious bread anymore."

The laughter died down as they all noticed a sullen-looking Jannik at the end of the table. Under the circumstances, the joke did seem a bit insensitive. Then one by one, the Woodlings said sorry to Max and then walked over to apologize and console Jannik. The apologies made Max feel a bit better, plus it was good to see the Woodlings laughing and coming together as a group, even if it was at his expense and insensitive to Jannik.

A Technological Solution

That night as he climbed into bed for some much-needed sleep, his mind began to wander. There was talk of leaving on a rescue mission for Moritz tomorrow, and he didn't know if he would be going or not. Although it was stressful to think about and he was tired from helping around the bakery all day, he tried to focus on remembering the most fun he had ever had. Maybe an idea for a toy would come to him this way. His mind immediately went to the video game *War of the Planets* and an assortment of other games he had played over the years. They were certainly fun, but looking back, they didn't fill him with the same feeling of joy that he got from actually doing fun stuff. His mind wandered to memories of going to the zoo with his parents or riding his bike for the first time. Max reflected back to when his family went to the beach in Virginia, spending all day playing in the waves on boogie boards, and most recently, riding the carousel at the Christmas market with his dad.

Sadness came over him. *My dad.* He found himself wishing for more fun things to come in the future. Then it hit him. A realization so clear and obvious that it had to be the answer. He had to figure out a way to get kids back to experiences like this! Activities like basketball, riding bikes, drawing pictures, shooting bows and arrows, snow sledding and all the other stuff he had forgotten. Still, Max didn't think kids would go for this. They wouldn't give up their computers and video games to ride bikes or catch frogs. No, something would have to make them give it up, and a new toy wasn't the answer. Then it dawned on him. That's it! They needed to create a computer virus.

Chapter 17:

The Nachtkrapp

Now he was having even more trouble getting to sleep. The thoughts were buzzing in his head at warp speed. All of a sudden, there was a knock at his cabin door. When Max opened the door, he saw an unfamiliar Woodling with a large black bird perched on his shoulders in the doorway. The bird was so large that it was the same size as the Woodling it was perched on. As they barged their way into the room, the Woodling spoke.

"Santa thought you might need some help getting to sleep." No sooner were the words spoken than the Woodling promptly left the cabin without saying another one. So it was just Max and this bird, and suddenly the situation felt very awkward. Its feathers were the color of black night and were those ... yes, they were! Arms! That Woodling had let a Nachtkrapp into his room! Quickly Max backed into the corner of the cabin, looking for something to grab. The fire poker would work. Max raised the poker to strike but was stopped by something. It was a noise. A beautiful, soothing noise. In fact, Max had never heard a more angelic sound in his entire life. It was coming from the Nachtkrapp, who was singing. Peace quickly came over Max, and he became sleepy. He couldn't let himself fall asleep! What would this thing do to him? It was useless, though; he couldn't resist. The beautiful sound had defeated him. He didn't recall falling asleep, but he remembered his dream again.

He was in school, listening to Fraulein Heimlich bark her instructions. He twisted his head to look around the room. Every one of the other kids was a Darkling! Fraulein Heimlich didn't seem to notice, and all the Darklings were paying attention to her every word. Their beady black eyes were following every sentence she wrote on the blackboard. Then Max leaned over to the one seated closest to him and said, "What did you get for number eight?" The creature turned to him, revealing dark, soulless eyes, and hissed. Then it screeched an awful, earsplitting noise. It was so loud that it woke Max up. That was all he could remember. It was a scary dream, and it filled Max with an uneasy feeling.

In the morning, Max woke up and discovered he was fine. The Nachtkrapp was gone and, for some reason, hadn't harmed him. He quickly turned his attention to finding Santa to share his idea from the night before. Someone else must have come into his cabin while he was sleeping because there was some bread, cheese, hot cocoa and a note on the table near the fireplace. The note read,

"Sorry if the Guter Nachtkrapp scared you last night. I thought you could use some help getting to sleep, and there is nothing better than the sound of the Guter Nachtkrapp for restless minds!" -Santa." This must have been a friendly version of the creature

Santa had mentioned in the woods. Noticing that the fire had died out in the night and the room was cold, Max quickly put on his boots, grabbed the plate of food and the cup of cocoa and left the cabin. Santa wasn't at his cabin, so Max walked down the hill to the dining hall. No one was in the dining hall, either. Max realized how quiet it was. Something was wrong. BOOM! CRAAACCKK! A massive ball of fire exploded in a fir tree next to him! He hit the snow and covered his head as sparks rained down around him. BOOM! He looked up and saw another fireball streak across the sky, headed right for the Christmas tree in the center of town! But when it was just about to hit the tree, it slammed into a blue force field. Max got up and ran down the hill until the fortress wall came into view. There he saw the Woodlings gathered along the wall ramparts. They were under attack!

Chapter 18:

Krampus at the Gates

"Max!" cried Jannik. "Come with me!" Max followed Jannik to the edge of the wall. Santa was there, looking out from over the castle ramparts. Max scaled the stairs up to the turret, where he saw an evil army of Darklings, at least a hundred of them. Dozens of dark birds that Max assumed must be the bad Nachtkrapp were perched on tall spikes. There were catapults, swords and spears encircling the castle walls like an army of death. At the head of the army, Krampus stood staring at them.

"How did they find us?!" yelled Jannik.

"Look!" Max shouted. "It's Moritz!" Except it wasn't Moritz. He had turned into one of Krampus's creatures. He was gray and shriveled, his eyes were cold and black, and he appeared to be chained to Krampus.

"Oh, Brother, what have they done to you?!" cried Jannik.

"He must have shown Krampus the way," Max said. Then a loud voice came from the battlefield below.

"Weihnachtsmann!" It was Krampus. "Today you will pay for your betrayal! Today is the end of you, Weihnachtsmann!"

"Santa, what are we going to do?" one of the Woodlings yelled. Santa didn't respond. He stood for a moment in silence as if nothing going on around him mattered. Krampus ran up and down the battle line, swatting the Darklings with sticks to get them fired up. Catapulted fireballs continued to rain down, chipping away at the fortress walls.

"I have an idea," Santa finally said. As he spoke, he looked directly at Max. Max got a sick feeling in the pit of his stomach, as he knew he was about to do something extremely dangerous.

Santa explained, "Legend has it that Krampus has only one known weakness. The Yule Lutzelfrau witch mentioned an idea to me in private that just might be perfect for this situation. It's never been proven, but it's our only hope."

"Well, what is it?" cried Jannik.

"Max, I need you to give Krampus an item for me. Do you see this orange?" An orange appeared in Santa's hand as if out of nowhere. Max was speechless. So many thoughts were running through his head. Finally, unable to speak, Max hesitantly nodded.

"This orange may have the power to rid us of Krampus," explained Santa. "It is said that Krampus cannot refuse a piece of fruit from a human child. He must accept it, eat it and then leave. He may not know that a human child is here today. Will you help us, Max?"

Max looked at the Woodlings and then at Santa, their faces long and desperate, and he could sense how much they needed his help.

"Okay, I'll do it," he said reluctantly.

"I will use transfusion to get you right in front of Krampus, so he doesn't have time to see you coming," said Santa. "Are you ready?" He looked at Max with anticipation.

"No!" Max half-screamed.

"Good," Santa said. Max took the orange from Santa's hand and closed his eyes. Santa raised his arms, and the blue light enveloped Max. He disappeared and reappeared right in front of Krampus and his Darkling army! Max's palms were so sweaty that the orange almost slipped out of his hands. Krampus was shocked. His look of surprise soon gave way to a curled smile. Where there wasn't coarse hair, his skin was a brownish-gray, and his horns were sharpened to a fine point, their ridges scarred with dents. His eyes were soulless, bursting with an evil intensity that Max had never seen outside of a villain in a scary movie. But this was no movie. This was happening! This was real!

Without thinking and keeping his eyes closed, Max thrust his hand out to reveal the piece of fruit. Krampus let out a noise that sounded like a cross between a howl and a scream. Max half-opened his eyes and saw Krampus staring at the orange, fighting with every ounce of strength to keep from grabbing it out of his hand. Max closed his eyes again and felt a hairy-clawed hand pick the orange from his. It was slow and felt like a piece of leather that had been left outside in the cold to freeze. Max didn't dare open his eyes. But he could smell him, hear him and feel him. After a few moments, he opened his eyes. Krampus was about a hundred yards away, walking from the battlefield, the Darklings at his side. It had worked!

Chapter 19:

The plan to save Christmas

Max had meant to mention to Santa that he could use a new pair of clothes, as it had been weeks since he'd changed his. None of the Woodlings or Santa seemed to be concerned with the necessary day-to-day things like brushing their teeth, bathing or doing laundry. Fortunately, Max had learned to fend for himself on such matters since his mom had been out of the picture for so long, and it wasn't a surprise that his dad wasn't very good at this sort of thing. However, the encounter with Krampus had accelerated his problem. As he watched Krampus walking from the battlefield, he felt warm liquid running down his leg. Although embarrassing for sure, he didn't think anyone could be faulted for doing the same if they found themselves in this situation. He would figure something out when he got back to his cabin.

As he walked back to the castle ramparts, the gate opened, and Santa and the Woodlings were all there, cheering wildly. Max had become their hero. He was able to return to his cabin where he was glad to see that the Woodlings had put out a new pair of pants for him. They felt warm when he put them on, like they had just come out of the dryer. *How could this be?* He wondered. Was it some sort of Woodling magic? It would have to remain a mystery for now because he was due back at the main hall for dinner. The mood at dinner was much more festive this time and they feasted for hours.

"Three cheers for Max!" cried one of the Woodlings.

"Were you scared?" Frauka asked.

"Did he say anything?" another Woodling inquired. Max was enjoying the attention, but out of the corner of his eye, he could see Santa sitting quietly. He wasn't sad or upset, but he didn't look happy or as spirited as the Woodlings. He looked lost in thought. When the festivities died down, Max approached him to see what he was thinking.

"What's wrong, Santa?" he asked.

"We have won the day, Max, and we have you to thank for this. But Krampus will be back. He still has Moritz, and he knows where our village is now. He won't rest until I'm finished, and Christmas along with me. With only three days until Christmas Eve, we have to think of a plan to save Christmas and stop Krampus."

"Santa!" Max exclaimed. "I have an idea for both!" He explained his computer virus idea to Santa and could see the light coming back to his face. He asked that Max explain it to Jannik, and Max began telling them about his idea. "You see, I figure that if we could come up with a virus that affected only the processor part of tablets, phones and game systems, kids would have no choice but to play with toys and other stuff."

"This could work, Max. It's so simple, I'm surprised no one has thought of it before," said Jannik. "But it would probably only last for a little while until the humans figured out how to block the virus."

"That's okay. Maybe all we need is some time to break the cycle with kids," Max said. "A couple months of playing with toys and playing outside could give Santa enough power to defeat Krampus for good!"

"Jannik, can you make it happen?" asked Santa.

"Christmas is coming quick, but I should be able to come up with something," Jannik replied.

"Now we just need to find a way to deliver it, and I think I know how," said Santa. "We need to get the virus into the system. Although we have power for computers here, we don't have internet access. Max, I will need you to return to the outside world."

They went over the plan several times and then returned to their cabins for much-needed rest. Max lay in bed that night, thinking about all sorts of things. *If the plan works*, he wondered, *will Christmas be saved? When I finally return home, will my dad still be there?* Home. He hadn't thought about going home for some time. He didn't really have a home that felt like home. But home was his dad. Home was the same racecar bed he'd had since he was four. Home was their cat, Wilbur. Suddenly, Max was tremendously homesick. *Will I tell Dad about where I've been?* The day's events and his encounter with Krampus had him wired. So, he started packing, but he didn't have much stuff. He would miss it here. He had never felt so alive, so important.

Chapter 20:

Christmas Chemistry

Max decided to take a walk that night. The moon was again shining down on a fresh blanket of snow, illuminating everything around him. The peace and quiet slowed his racing mind. He passed the great hall, now quiet after all the Woodlings had left for their own beds. Out in front of Santa's cabin, he could see smoke hanging on the porch. The moonlight was shining on the silhouette of a figure. Santa was smoking his pipe again.

"Santa?" Max said hesitantly.

"Good evening, Max," said Santa. "I see you couldn't sleep either. The excitement of the day would be a lot for any child to handle. Krampus is growing weaker. I sense it. We must hurry before he returns now that he knows you are here, as well as knowing the way here."

"He has so many Darklings on his side, though!" Max said.

"Sadly, yes, but I hope not for much longer. You see, most of the Darklings were once children! Children of weak mind and whose imaginations have been dulled are the most susceptible. After being spirited away to Krampus's lair, they stop growing and begin to let the evil overtake their souls until they are owned entirely by Krampus." Santa continued, "Even though some things come from an innocent place, they can turn dark fast. Although Krampus doesn't have Christmas magic or physical powers, he has exceptional mind-control powers and the ability to transform the souls of children. Now they do his bidding, and I have to figure out a way to save them."

This is why they looked so familiar, Max thought. *They aren't troll-like creatures. Most of them were kids just like me! But Moritz isn't a kid, and he's a Darkling now.*

"Is there still a way to save Moritz?" Max asked.

"I'm not sure," replied Santa. Woodlings are different than children in that they are less susceptible to Krampus's magic. But once the magic takes complete hold, it is often permanent."

"You can do it, Santa. I believe in you," Max said. No sooner were those words spoken when a blue light faintly flickered on the end of Santa's staff.

"What was that?" Max asked.

"I grow stronger each day. Your belief in me or, rather, your belief in Christmas magic is how we can defeat Krampus and save the Darklings. Here, have a cookie," he said, handing a gingerbread cookie to Max.

"Santa?" Max asked with cookie crumbs falling out of his mouth. "Was there ever a Mrs. Claus?" Santa looked down, saying nothing at first. It seemed the question had caught him off-guard. After several awkward moments, Max spoke again. "Santa?"

"Yes, Max, there was," he finally said.

"What happened?"

"Krampus..." and Santa abruptly stopped himself. "You should get along to bed, young Max. You have a big day tomorrow." Max could tell Santa didn't want to speak about it, but he couldn't help wondering what had happened to Mrs. Claus. Was she dead? Walking back toward his cabin, he saw a light in the window of Frauka's cabin. He was curious as to why she was up so late and decided to knock.

"Oh, Max, it's just you," she said. "Come in, come in, I have something for you!" Her cabin was even messier than before, and books and jars were everywhere.

"First, I need your help," she said. "I'm making a potion that can give you the ability to disguise yourself as another living being. But I can't find the spell. It's in this book." She placed a gigantic book on the desk next to Max. "Look for the spell marked Chameleon Camouflage. I have to work on this other potion for you while there's still time." The book was bound in leather and looked very old, and it must have had a thousand pages. Max immediately went into boredom mode out of habit. He rarely looked at books. Reluctantly, he opened it and started to read. It was as boring as he thought, and he swore he could hear Fraulein Heimlich shouting in his ear with that hot, stinky breath, telling him to keep reading. Or his mom yelling at him to stop watching TV and pick up a book. He would just have to power through it.

The more he read, though, the more he found the various spells fascinating. One was for invisibility, one for wingless flight and even one for making farts smell like flowers! About an hour into the book, he finally came upon it.

"Yes! Yes! That's it, Max. Good work!" Frauka exclaimed. "Now hand me that. Now mix this. Turn up the temperature on that

Bunsen burner, won't you?" Frauka instructed. Max hurried to do as he was told until suddenly, POOF! A cloud of blue smoke flew up in his face. Frauka bent over, laughing hysterically.

"I got you, Max!" she yelled through the laughing. Max, looking like a Smurf, started laughing too.

"It will come off after about an hour, Max, don't worry. Just a little bit more, and we should be ready. Could you mix these two liquids together for me?"

Max was suspicious of her now and hesitated. "I promise no more jokes," Frauka insisted. He figured it was safe and mixed them together.

"There, do you see how this green liquid reacts to the other? All finished. Here you are, Max. Just drink it and think of the being you want to become. But don't forget that it wears off after several hours. Or is it several days?" She shook her head. "Oh well, I'll finish the containment and have it for you in the morning. In the meantime, take this other potion now."

"What is it?" Max asked.

"It's pure Christmas Magic!" Frauka replied.

"Well, how do I use it?"

"You will know when the time is right," she said. "I had Santa add a little something extra to it. Now off to bed with you." She shooed him out the door quickly, so he had no time to ask any more questions.

Chapter 21:

Back to Civilization

Max fell asleep rather quickly, and before he knew it, the morning had come. He had loaded a small backpack with snacks Chef Otto had made for him. There were soft, chewy pretzels, an apple and Lebkuchen gingerbread in it. The potions that Frauka had made for him would be the heaviest items. He walked down the path to the dining hall and into the sound of raucous cheer. He blushed and wished he could dive under a table, out of sight. The food and drink were passed around as Max took his seat. He was surprised to see a plate of breakfast burritos in front of him.

"Aren't they delicious?" one of the Woodlings commented. "Santa brought them back one Christmas from Mexico, and Otto makes them all the time now."

"Yes, and next week on the menu is spaghetti from Italy!" another Woodling announced with a grin. They all ate quickly and then Santa, Jannik and Max went over the plan.

"Use transfusion to enter the edge of town. Find the nearest computer, and download the virus using a zip drive," Jannik explained.

Sounds easy enough, Max thought. The only hard part would be that they couldn't use transfusion to return him until he was within sight of Santa. He would have to walk back through part of the forest alone. The thought of this terrified Max, but they had thought long and hard on it and couldn't come up with a better solution. They finished their breakfast and walked toward the castle gate.

"Max, if you want to stay in the real world after your mission is complete, I will understand," Santa said, looking at him with compassion.

Max didn't know what to say. The thought of staying hadn't crossed his mind. But the thought of lazy Saturday afternoons playing video games and eating pizza did sound appealing. And he did miss his dad an awful lot. Plus, he wouldn't have to walk back through the woods alone.

"Okay," was the only word his overwhelmed brain could think of to say. Frauka was walking with them as well. She walked over to the Christmas tree in the center of town and clipped off a small branch.

"Here, from Der Tannenbaum," she said. Max looked at her oddly, and she explained, "For luck."

When they approached the castle gate, Santa asked, "Are you ready, Max?"

"Yes, I think so," Max replied. Santa again raised his arms and staff over his head, and the blue light enveloped Max. Instantly, he was standing at the edge of the forest, looking at the half-timbered buildings at the edge of Dinkelstadt. He could see the people in the

Christmas market stalls setting up their items for sale. The church bells were ringing from the cathedral in the town center as if to say, "Guten morgen!" It felt strange to be back in the real world and see so many people bustling around. Max quickly scanned the buildings to see if one would suit his needs. The tourist information center caught his eye, and he walked over to see if they had any computers. It was quiet inside, and Max was the only person there other than a woman behind the counter.

"Frohliche Weihnachten, kann ich ihnen helfen?" she asked.

"Uh ... I need to use a computer," Max said.

"Oh, yes, there is one over there in the corner," she said in English this time, pointing to the computer. She looked at him in a perplexed way. Max quickly approached the computer and got started. He plugged in the zip drive and used the computer mouse to highlight the "start download" task. The computer prompted him: "Do you want to download the contents of this external drive?" Max suddenly realized the significance of what he was about to do. *I love online games. Am I really about to destroy them?* He was surprised at how easy the decision was. There was no turning back now. Helping Santa and the Woodlings save Christmas was the only thing on his mind.

Chapter 22:

Discovered by Darklings

Max hit the button, and the computer started downloading its contents.

"Do you need any assistance?" asked the woman.

Max jumped. "No, thank you," he said nervously. It would take a few minutes for the download to finish, and he didn't want any interruptions. As he waited, he looked out the window and saw something out of the corner of his eye. It was a poster on a lamppost. It had a picture of him with large letters that said "MISSING!" His eyes shifted down the street, and he saw someone putting up another poster on the side of a building. It was his dad! Max immediately felt the urge to run outside and hug him, but something stopped him. If he did, he wouldn't be able to help Santa. His dad wouldn't let him out of his sight for a minute, let alone let him return to Santa's village. His dad wouldn't understand.

Just then, the woman interrupted his thoughts as she spoke up. "Hey! You're that boy everyone is looking for!"

Shocked that he had been discovered, Max blurted out, "No I'm not." He glanced at the computer. Ninety-seven percent complete.

"Yes, it's you!" the woman continued. "I'm calling the police. Stay right there."

Ninety-nine percent complete.

"I promise, it's not me," Max said, trying to sound convincing.

Come on! 100% complete! Max grabbed the zip drive and ran out of the tourist office as the woman was shouting, "Halt! Halt!"

He quickly ran across the street and made a dash for the edge of the forest, running as fast as he could. He ran for some time and then finally took a break to catch his breath. He hadn't even noticed that he was in the middle of the forest now.

It was daytime, but the evergreen woods were so thick that it felt much later in the day and seemed almost dark. Rays of sun shone through the treetop canopy in spots, hitting the forest floor and creating steam that appeared as smoke rising. A sick feeling came over him as he realized he didn't know which way was which. As the steam on the ground shifted and swirled, he could see the distinct outline of a person's hand! Then another nearby! Before he knew it, he was surrounded by a multitude of zombie hands clawing their way to the surface! Just as his heart began to pump uncontrollably, he noticed they weren't moving. Everything was perfectly still. Taking a brave step closer, he knelt down to look more closely. They weren't hands. *But what are they?* With even more courage, he touched one of the objects. It was a fungus! A fungus that looked just like a human zombie hand!

"Hoooot ... Hoooot ... Hoot." An owl in a nearby tree sang out, cutting the silence. *That's it; I'm outta here,* he thought. It was all too much, and he had to keep moving. He wandered for a while, looking for the castle walls but couldn't find anything. Then he heard noises coming from behind a group of large boulders. He crept up to the edge and peered around the corner. Darklings! At least a dozen of them. No sooner had he seen them than one of the Darklings pointed right at him and screeched that horrible scream. *I'm doomed!* He quickly turned around to run but saw another group coming from behind him! They hadn't seen him yet. *What to do?* Thinking quickly, he grabbed the Chameleon Camouflage potion from his backpack and drank from the bottle. "Darkling," he thought to himself. No sooner had he finished drinking the potion than the group of Darklings from behind was upon him.

"Where is the boy? Find him!" one of them wailed. Then he crept closer to Max. "What are you doing away from your group?" he asked in a raspy, hissing voice.

"Nothing," Max replied. The creature drew closer still as if inspecting every inch of Max, sniffing his hair and skin. He was larger than the others and had long, black hair along with his horns. Max was terrified but found himself inspecting the Darkling as well, looking for any signs of the child who might still be in there.

"Get back to your group now and keep looking for the boy!" the Darkling snarled. It appeared the potion had worked. Max looked down at his arms. They were gray and pale, and his face felt rough and leathery. He was a Darkling!

Chapter 23:

Krampus's Lair

"Keep searching for the boy!" one of the Darklings yelled. Max figured his best chance of survival for now was to follow a group of Darklings through the forest in hopes that they would lead him somewhere familiar. Then again, he didn't really have a choice. It felt strange walking in their hunched-over manner, and he constantly looked for a recognizable landmark to present the right opportunity to leave the group and escape. After an hour or so, one of them shouted, "Back to the cave! The master demands it!"

Cave? Master? If he was going to make his move and escape, now was the time. Max waited till they turned a corner around a boulder and made sure he was at the back of the group. He quickly darted behind a rock but inadvertently stepped on a stick, and it snapped.

"Where are you going?" one of the Darklings turned around and hissed.

"Uh … nowhere," Max said under his breath.

"Back in line, you!" Max had no choice but to follow. Before he knew it, the chance to escape had vanished, and he was staring up at the entrance to a cave that looked like it could be the entrance to hell itself. Icicles hung from the cavern entrance ceiling, making it look like rows of teeth. It reminded him of those creepy fish that live in the deepest, darkest parts of the ocean and have those long, razor-sharp teeth. It was dark, cold and had a rotten stench that almost made Max gag. He could hear a faint drumming noise coming from the depths of the cavern. A few of the Darklings grabbed lanterns, and they began their descent into what Max knew could be none other than Krampus's lair.

They walked for some time. Down, down, down. They passed cages, some empty and some with children in them! Their terrified faces were dirty and wide-eyed. Some of the caged children had already begun to transform. A child had one horn on his head, and another had pale gray skin on her arms. Several Nachtkrapp were perched on top of the cages, picking at the captives through the bars. Max's heart started racing. The fear was almost too much for him, and he considered what might happen if he just made a run for it. A quick end to his life is what would happen, so he didn't give it another thought.

The drumming got louder and louder, and the small tunnel opened up to a large cavern. Torches illuminated the size of the room, as well as an enormous stone throne in the middle atop a pile of bones. There were at least fifty Darklings now. Some were drumming, others sharpening various weapons. All at once, the drumming stopped. It was eerily silent for a few moments. Then he heard a voice start in with a low growl.

"For five hundred years, we have waited. Five hundred years of persecution. Weihnachtsmann's power is weak. It is finally our time!" All of the Darklings cheered wildly. "This year ... This year will be the LAST Christmas!" Krampus suddenly came into full view, and again the Darklings cheered. Chains that were wrapped around Krampus's waist were dragging behind him, and his curved horns were as big and sharp as ever.

"Do we have the boy?" Krampus asked.

"No, master," one of the Darklings stepped forward and answered hesitantly. "He disappeared in the forest."

"Aaahh!" Krampus screamed in anger. "We must find him! You!" he said, pointing at one of the Darklings. "You will lead the search party at once." It was Moritz! Or, at least what used to be Moritz. *If I could only escape and bring Moritz back with me,* Max thought. "The rest of you, prepare your divisions for battle!" Krampus shouted. "Tomorrow is Christmas Eve!"

Then things got quiet all of a sudden. A nearby Darkling turned and looked at Max in bewilderment. Then another one began staring at him. Max looked down at his hands, and the gray hairy skin was gone. The Darklings were all staring in disbelief at him now. The magic potion had worn off!

Chapter 24:

Food Cage!

"Seize him!" Krampus yelled.

Max was captured. He felt the dread creep over him that he might actually die. Or worse yet, be turned into a Darkling.

"Shall we put him in a transformation cage or a food cage and prepare him for your dinner, Master?" one of the Darklings asked. A chant began to rise up in unison: "Eat! Eat! Eat! Eat!"

"Food cage! But we will let this one suffer first!" Krampus yelled. They took Max's backpack and dragged him to the corner of the cavern where there was a small iron-bar cage. They threw him inside, locking the door with a key.

"We have the boy!" shouted Krampus triumphantly. Then he began to slowly walk over to Max. The cheers from the Darklings died down as Krampus approached the cage. He got right next to the bars and stared directly at Max for several moments. His breath had the odor of rotting vegetables, and his sharp teeth were yellow and bloody.

"Who are you, boy?" he said quietly and curiously. Max didn't answer, as he was completely frozen with fear. Krampus began looking over every inch of Max and smelling the air around the cage.

"The Weihnachtsmann sent you, didn't he? Why? To try to stop me? To save his wife? She is someplace where he can never find her." Through the terror, it dawned on Max that Santa's wife was alive!

Max sheepishly spoke. "W..why do you want revenge on Santa anyways? He only banished you because you started eating kids."

"Is that all he told you?" Krampus said. "You poor, naïve fool. Did he tell you that I was once human? That I loved his wife too? No, of course he didn't. But she did not return my love and told me that she loved the Weihnachtsmann. It was Christmas Eve, and I will never forget it or forgive it. But now I have her. She will be mine forever." Max was stunned. Although Krampus had been turned into a horned devil-like beast that ate children and hated Christmas, he was once a man with a conscience and the ability to love!

"With your capture, the Weihnachtsmann's fate is sealed, and Christmas is finally finished," he said with an evil grin emerging on his thin lips. There was a commotion, and Max looked over and saw the Darklings fighting over his backpack. When one of them finally got it for himself, he opened it up and emptied the contents. The jar containing the Christmas magic potion fell onto the ground but did not break. The Darkling picked it up and studied it and then began to open it.

Krampus turned around and shrieked in horror, "NO! Don't open that!" A blue flash filled the cavern and blinded everyone for several seconds. When Max finally started to regain his vision,

FOOD CAGE!

what he saw shocked him. Kids. Woodlings. Dozens. Maybe forty or so. The Christmas magic had changed them all back! Krampus, realizing the situation, quickly fled the cavern. The children and Woodlings were all staring at one another in confusion. Then smiles slowly spread across their faces as they realized they had been freed.

"Max!" one of the Woodlings yelled. It was Moritz! He had been the Darkling with the key to the cage that Max was in and quickly opened it for him. "We're free, Max! Thank you! We must return to Santa at once to warn him."

"What about all of these children?" Max asked.

"We'll have to take them with us," replied Moritz. The children were still in a state of shock from finding themselves in human form again in some dark, smelly cave.

Max got up on the throne and began to shout. "Listen, all of you." You have been freed from Krampus's spell. Christmas Eve is tomorrow! Now let's get you back to your families. Follow me!" Max and Moritz began to lead them out of the cave when Max suddenly remembered ... Mrs. Claus.

"Moritz! We need to look for Mrs. Claus! Maybe she's in this cave!"

"She's not in the cave anymore, Max. I've been down here for a couple of weeks now and know every inch of this place. He's keeping her someplace else." The news was disappointing to Max, but they needed to focus on other tasks at the moment.

"How will we return all these kids to their parents?" Max wondered aloud. "Maybe Santa has an idea."

"It's worth a try," said Moritz. They continued on their way up and out of the cave. It would be morning soon, and Christmas Eve was finally here.

Chapter 25:
A Joyous Reunion

THE WALK THROUGH THE FOREST seemed to go on forever, but fortunately, Moritz knew the way. The dozens of children and several Woodlings seemed tired but in good spirits. Max was walking alongside Moritz and was happy to have a familiar being to talk to.

"Do you believe Krampus about all of that Mrs. Claus stuff?" Max asked.

"I don't remember everything from my time as a Darkling, but I remember that Krampus had her in the cave at some point," Moritz replied. "I believe that whatever feelings he may have had for her at one time have been replaced by evil and the need for revenge. Santa may know more about it."

After a couple of hours, they made it to the castle gate. The doors swung open, and all the Woodlings cheered their return. Their mood was happy, and the often-gloomy looks on many of their faces were all smiles now. Santa was there, too, and his smile was the most welcome sight of all. The children were awestruck by the scene. Seeing it brought Max back to the first time he met Santa and entered the village. But the Christmas tree in the center of town was now decorated with the most beautiful ornaments and colored lights. All of the Woodlings' huts were strung with glistening lights and wreaths on the doors, and the falling snow made it the most enchanting Christmas scene ever.

"Moritz!" yelled Jannik.

"Brother!" exclaimed Moritz. They embraced and cried tears of joy and relief. Max went over to Santa and gave him a big hug as well.

"You did great, Max! The computer virus worked! The humans will ultimately fix the virus, but for now, parents are scrambling, and the wishes have been flooding in for toys! My power is almost fully restored and at the perfect time with Christmas Eve tonight. You all must be hungry. Let's feast!" exclaimed Santa, overwhelmed with gratitude and joy.

"Santa?" Max inquired. "We were hoping you had an idea for how to help the children who have been freed from Krampus's curse."

"Yes, I think I do, Max. I think I know just what to do. Let us eat and drink and then it's back to work preparing for the big night ahead of us." The children were assured of their return to their families and fed a buffet of delicious Christmas treats ... gingerbread, candy canes, chocolate, hot cocoa, cookies and so much more! Max stuffed himself as well.

"Come, Max," Santa said. "Can you help me pack the sleigh?"

"Absolutely!" Max replied.

They spent the better part of the day packing and preparing the reindeer. There were so many toys! Superhero figures,

Princess doll figures, Legos, remote-controlled cars, *War of the Planets* foam dart guns. Everything a kid could want.

"How are you going to get toys to all the kids in the world?" Max asked.

"Well, I make lots of trips ... and a little Christmas magic doesn't hurt too," Santa said with a smile. "Here, take these pails to the stable and help me feed the reindeer."

The food in the pails was glowing blue this time. "Magic food?" Max asked excitedly.

"So they can fly, of course!" exclaimed Santa.

As night fell, they fed the reindeer and then returned to their cabins to get ready for the big night ahead of them. All the children were still eating and laughing at the dining hall when Max changed clothes and walked down to Santa's cabin. Santa was stoking the embers in the fireplace and didn't notice Max at first.

"Krampus told me about Mrs. Claus," Max said. Santa immediately became still, and all Max could hear was the crackling of the burning wood. "Is it true?"

Santa breathed a big sigh. "It is," he replied sadly. "He could not control his anger over her rejection of him, and the hate consumed him. Now he has her, and I don't know where she is or if she is even alive anymore." Santa's eyes were downcast, and it saddened Max to see the joyous light missing from Santa's eyes.

CHAPTER 26:

THE SLEIGH

"SHE IS ALIVE, SANTA," SAID MAX. "We didn't see her or find out where Krampus is keeping her, but he told us she is somewhere hidden."

Santa's spirits seemed to brighten with this news, but he still hung his head again.

"I love her, and she is the only family that I have," he finally said.

"That's not true, Santa. The Woodlings are your family, and I am now too! In fact, all the children of the world are your family!" As Max said this, Santa nodded his head listening.

"We could go back to his lair and look for her; Moritz knows the way," Max suggested.

"No, she's not there," replied Santa. "I don't know how I'm ever going to find her."

"We'll find her, Santa," Max said emphatically. "We can't give up now."

"Santa?" Max asked. "When I was in the cave in Krampus's lair, the potion of Christmas magic that Frauka made for me was opened, and that's what turned all the Darklings back into children. How come it didn't change Krampus back into his human form?"

"The potion only works on those who still have belief buried deep in their heart. Belief in Christmas," said Santa. "I had hoped that there was still this belief in Krampus's twisted black heart, but alas, it would seem not so. Enough talk, Max. It is time. Christmas is here."

The sleigh was super cool. It was red with gold trim and big cushy seats. The wood designs and trim were impressive, and Max wondered who had made it, as it looked quite old. The back part of the sleigh was overstuffed with a large canvas bag filled with toys. It would take all night and many trips, but it was so exciting to see Santa step into the sleigh with a big smile on his face. The Woodlings and children were gathered round the Christmas tree, laughing and cheering. Max could feel the energy buzzing in the air all around. Then Santa pulled him aside.

"Your help has been invaluable to me, Max. I was wondering if you might join me on my sleigh tonight?"

Max was speechless at first but then shouted loudly, "YES! AWESOME!" He climbed aboard, and Santa snapped the reigns.

"Hiyah!" Santa shouted, and they were off! At first, the sleigh glided on the freshly fallen snow and then began climbing higher and higher into the sky. Max had to pinch himself. He was flying in Santa's sleigh on Christmas Eve! The reindeer were running on air led by Humbo and Bumbo in the front. They circled back around and waved to the Woodlings and children below.

"Ho, ho, ho! Merry Christmas!" Santa shouted in classic Santa form. The sleigh had some sort of warp speed because before Max knew it, they were in North America! They got to work quickly. Santa brought out his thick book containing all the names of the children and what toys they wanted.

Their landing on the first roof was as smooth as silk. Santa raised his staff, and they used transfusion to enter the home. A beautiful Christmas tree was in the corner, all lit up. They quickly filled the stockings then put the presents quietly under the tree. Santa was looking around the room for something.

"What is it?" Max whispered.

"I'm looking for the milk and cookies," replied Santa. "Ah, here they are." He gave Max a cookie and began drinking the milk.

"Shouldn't we get back to the …" Max began.

"Shh shh shh," Santa interrupted. "*Always* take time for milk and cookies."

Max took a moment to clear his head and enjoy the sweet chocolate in his mouth. Santa wrote a quick note to thank the kids for the treats and then he gave the word, and it was back up to the sleigh and on to the next house. They saw all manner of homes and apartments. Some people didn't have a Christmas tree at all. Other homes were very poor with only a dirt floor and no running water, but they still had decorations up. Some were lavish mansions. One stop wasn't a house or an apartment; it was an orphanage. Max had heard of these places but was now getting an up-close look at what life without any parents at all looked like. There wasn't a Christmas tree, but Santa took the time to carefully place a present on the bunk bed of every child. Max suddenly felt very fortunate about his own life that he had completely taken for granted up until now.

Chapter 27:
Delivering Presents

To save time at some houses and apartments, Santa used transfusion to teleport the presents into the homes. But it seemed as though he knew which houses had the best milk and cookies because he made sure to personally visit those homes. He must have eaten thirty cookies and drank ten glasses of milk! A couple of times, they heard noises banging around upstairs in bedrooms, and a few children ran down the stairs to try and catch a glimpse of Santa. But he heard them coming and was out of there with the snap of a finger. He was sneaky! Most of the homes were in Europe and the Americas, but some were on other continents … Africa and Asia and even Australia and Antarctica. It was especially cold there, but somehow Max stayed warm with all the excitement around. He wondered if the sleigh had some kind of heating mechanism, as it never froze and seemed warm every time he got in. It was more fun than he could have possibly imagined. Giving gifts like hoverboards, toy robots, toy unicorns, drones and all sorts of other toys gave him a warm feeling inside. After several hours of this, as well as many return trips to the village to get more presents, they returned to refuel the reindeer and take a short break.

"Now, Max, it's time to return the children," said Santa.

"But we aren't done with all the presents," replied Max.

"Don't worry, I will finish the rest of the presents later." They returned to the village and took several children at a time.

The kids hung their faces over the edge of the sleigh railing, watching the towns below and the stars above. Their looks of wonderment were undeniable. They had no idea what was going on, but they didn't seem overly scared. When they got to the first house, Santa took one of the small girls by the hand. They transfused into the living room, and Santa got down on his knees to talk to the girl.

"Merry Christmas, Sara," he said in German as he blew into his hands. Sparkling dust flew into the girl's face, temporarily stunning her. They hid and watched as the girl regained her awareness and began yelling for her parents. The parents came rushing down the stairs and fell to their knees, hugging her and crying.

"They have been without their daughter for over a year and have searched and searched for her," whispered Santa. "She won't remember anything," he added. Max was sad for a moment that the girl wouldn't have any memory of her magical sleigh ride with Santa. But being with her family instead of trapped in the body of a Darkling in Krampus's lair was obviously the best life for her. The reunion was emotional, and her parents were peppering her with questions she didn't have the answers to. But Max couldn't help but think of the empty cages he saw in Krampus's lair and the stories about him eating children. Some parents would not get to enjoy such a blissful reunion with their child, and some children would return to parents who were much older.

Max's sadness would have to take a back seat, though, as there were still lots of kids to return. They transfused back up to the sleigh, and over the next several hours, they returned each child home.

"There's just one child left," Santa said in a solemn tone.

The sleigh was empty, and Max didn't think there were any more kids at Santa's village. He looked at Santa, confused for a moment. Santa smiled back at him. *Oh wait, it is me.* It made Max feel sad and excited at the same time. Santa didn't say anything and just kept smiling. Max's adventure had come to an end.

Chapter 28:

An Unwelcome Surprise

As they were taking off from the roof of the last house, they suddenly felt a huge jarring sensation on the sleigh and heard a loud crash! Terror gripped them both as they turned to see Krampus standing at the back of the sleigh! He had jumped on from the rooftop, and now he was flying with them. His eyes were glowing that unmistakable, terrifying red color. His arms were outstretched with his claws engaged. His body was lunging with each breath as if consumed and empowered with rage and hate. He began climbing over the seats toward them and then swiped at Max.

The claws cut into Max's arm, and blood immediately started oozing from the wound. It burned, and Max fell into the front seat of the sleigh, clutching his arm. Santa pointed his staff at Krampus, and a bolt of blue light shot right into his chest, knocking him backward. Krampus slowly got back up and resumed his approach. Santa was about ready to fire another shot when Krampus sprung forth and knocked the staff out of Santa's hands. Then he landed a massive punch to Santa's head. Santa crumpled to the floor of the sleigh.

"NOOO!" shouted Max, and intense anger immediately began swelling inside him. A rage that had been growing within him for years. He suddenly burst forward and lunged at Krampus, pushing with all his strength against the cold, gray body. It caught Krampus by surprise, and he lost his balance and fell over the sleigh railing! Max got back up on his feet and looked over the edge. There was Krampus, hanging from the runners underneath. Looking past him, Max could see the clouds flying by at great speed, and Krampus was grabbing for the edge of the sleigh railing. Max looked back, and Santa was coming to but still in quite a daze. Max looked around for something to grab. The bag of presents had spilled, and there on the floor of the sleigh was a *War of the Planets* foam dart gun, just like his at home. Without hesitating, he grabbed it and shot a dart at Krampus, hitting him right in the forehead. It harmlessly bounced off Krampus, who snarled and yelled at Max while trying to reach the railing.

"Think, Max!" he commanded himself.

"Max, give me the gun," mumbled Santa, barely able to sit up. Max handed Santa the toy dart gun. He cupped his hands around the dart chamber, and a blue light began to glow. He handed it back to Max, who pointed the gun at Krampus again, but this time, Max wasn't afraid. Krampus saw it, and a look of fear overcame his face. Max fired the shot, and the glowing blue dart found its mark, knocking Krampus from the sleigh. As if in slow motion, Krampus fell into the clouds below, screaming, as Max watched from the sleigh. Then Krampus instantly disappeared. He was gone. They were so high up that he couldn't have survived. *Could he?*

An Unwelcome Surprise

Max went over and helped Santa to his feet. Sadly, Santa shook his head from side to side and cried, "She's gone, and I'll never find her now."

"We don't know that," said Max. "We've come too far and accomplished too much to give up now."

"I hope you're right, Max. But first, let's get back to the village to treat your wound before it gets worse."

When they got back to the village, the Woodlings were curious and concerned for both Max and Santa and immediately began tending to their injuries. Max's arm still hurt pretty badly, and he would need stitches to close the wound. For a moment, he worried that he might have some kind of zombie-like infection that would turn him into a Krampus-like creature. But his fears evaporated when Santa came over and placed his hands on the wound. That familiar blue glow was cool to the touch. It penetrated his skin and soothed the pain.

Max could feel the difference in Santa; he was strong now. Stronger than ever. News spread of Krampus's demise, and the Woodlings were overjoyed. They had to hurry, though, as they were quickly losing time, and Santa still had a lot of toys to deliver. Moritz and Jannik came over to Max before he got back on the sleigh.

"Thank you, Max. We owe you our lives. We will never forget you," they said.

"I'll never forget you either," replied Max. As he said that, he hoped Santa would allow him to remember everything, unlike the other kids.

CHAPTER 29:
THE MEANING OF CHRISTMAS SPIRIT

THE TWO OF THEM TOOK OFF INTO THE NIGHT SKY again and headed toward Max's apartment. When they got there, they transfused into his family room. It was surreal for Max to be back at the apartment. So much had happened to him since the last time he saw it. A small fake Christmas tree was in the corner with a few ornaments on it. He thought of his dad, trying his best to raise him, missing him, looking for him, yet still managing to put up a tree. He missed his dad so much. Santa was off in a corner, grumbling about "no cookies," and Max had to laugh a bit inside. Max felt something rub up against his leg and looked down to see his cat Wilbur purring with delight at Max's return. Max scratched him in all the right spots.

Then Santa came over and got down on his knees in front of Max.

"I have to leave now, Max. I must continue my search for Mrs. Claus, but I want to thank you. You've saved Christmas, and you will forever have a place in my heart."

"I may have helped save Christmas, but you saved me," Max replied with tears in his eyes. He gave Santa a great big hug. "I'm ready. You can make me forget now," said Max.

Santa looked into Max's eyes. "No, Max, not you. You must never forget." Max was visibly crying now. "Do you still want *War of the Planets 2* for Christmas?" Santa asked.

"What I really want is my mom and dad back," Max said.

Santa placed his hand on Max's shoulder and said, "I'll see what I can do, Max. Don't give up hope. I have a feeling you may get what you want for Christmas someday." As he said this, he winked at Max. This excited and confused Max, but he tried to pay attention to Santa's words. "Don't forget that I will always be with you," Santa continued. "Do you know what Christmas spirit is now?" Max nodded.

"Christmas spirit is the courage to do the right thing," said Santa. "Christmas spirit is putting aside your fears and worries and helping those in need. It is experiencing all this world has to offer. It is joy, it is family, and it is a reward for a hard day's work. It is the feeling you get from giving rather than getting, and it is love. Now take what you have learned and use it in your life."

Max understood. He felt like a completely different person since this all started, and he was grateful.

"Look at your fingers, Max," Santa said. Max hadn't realized it, but his fingernails were long and smooth. He stared at them for a few moments, smiling with a sense of inner pride.

"Goodbye, Santa," Max said.

"Oh, but it's not goodbye forever, just goodbye for now," said

Santa with a gleam in his eye. Max looked at him, wondering what he meant. And then, just like that, he was gone.

Max wiped the tears from his eyes and then called out, "Dad! Dad!" He heard a noise in the back bedroom like someone tripping over furniture, and suddenly, Max's dad was standing in the hallway, a look of astonishment on his face. He ran to Max, and they hugged so hard it nearly suffocated him. The feeling of love washed over him as they cried tears of joy.

"Merry Christmas, Dad," Max said.

"Where have you been, Max!?" his dad asked.

Thinking quickly, Max started fibbing. "It's a long story. I fell and hit my head on some ice when we were in Dinkelstadt. When I came to, everyone was gone. I thought I knew the way home, but the fall must have confused me. I ended up in a forest, lost for days and days. I finally made it out and eventually here," Max said.

"Weren't you cold? What did you eat? Where did you hit your head? Maybe we should take you to the doctor…" Max's dad began to ask him a ton of questions, but Max just interrupted him.

"Dad, I'm just tired, cold and hungry. Can we talk about it later?"

"I've been worried sick!" his dad exclaimed. "Yes, of course. All that matters is that you're back. It's a Christmas miracle! Let's get you warmed up and fed. I'm sorry I don't have any presents for you, I just thought…"

"What do you mean? It doesn't look like you forgot," said Max, pointing to the tree that now had presents underneath it.

"Did you bring those?" his dad asked.

"No, it wasn't me," said Max. "I could barely get myself here." They looked at each other for a few seconds and then shrugged their shoulders and went over to the tree. They opened presents and laughed and hugged some more. When Max got to the last present, he opened it, and there was a *War of the Planets* foam dart gun!

"Oh, you already have one of those someplace," said his dad. "That's too bad. Maybe we can give it to a needy child or something."

Max looked closely and could see a faint blue glowing light coming from the dart chamber!

"No," Max said confidently, "I think I'll keep this one."

The End

About the Author

DEVIN ARLOSKI is a sales and marketing specialist, children's fiction author, and kid at heart, who lives and plays in Longmont, Colorado with his wife, two sons, dog, and two cats. He graduated from Colorado State University in 1997 and his first middle grade novel is The Christmas Curse of Krampus. A tale of a young boy who encounters the legendary beast, Krampus, and winds up helping the real Santa Claus try to defeat him and save Christmas along with his own belief in Christmas magic.

    He recently went with his wife and two young sons to Germany and France to visit the famous Christmas markets and was inspired by their beauty and tradition, as well as local folklore. His eldest son is 10 years old and prolonging his belief in Christmas and the magic of the Christmas season is part of the impetus for writing his first novel. His mission is to bring reading joy to kids and parents interested in Christmas magic and international folklore, and his creativity is what drives him to produce stories that have yet to be told. His website for his first novel is www.thechristmascurseofkrampus.com

Made in the USA
Middletown, DE
08 January 2022